RAVEN

A TRICKSTER TALE FROM
THE PACIFIC NORTHWEST

TOLD AND ILLUSTRATED BY

Gerald McDermott

SCHOLASTIC INC.

New York   Toronto   London   Auckland   Sydney

ISBN 0-590-48249-1

Copyright © 1993 by Gerald McDermott. All rights reserved. Published by Scholastic Inc., 555 Broadway, New York, N.Y. 10012, by arrangement with Harcourt Brace Publishers.

12 11 10 9 8 7 6 5 4 3 2   4 5 6 7 8 9/9

Printed in the U.S.A.   37

First Scholastic printing, January 1994

The paintings in this book were done in gouache, colored pencil, and pastel on heavyweight cold-press watercolor paper.

Along the coast of the Pacific Northwest, as far north as Alaska, Raven is the central character in most Native American myths and tales. A shape-shifter imbued with magical powers, he is at once brave and cunning, greedy and gluttonous. Raven is a trickster on a cosmic scale, mischief-maker, and culture hero, at times wreaking havoc and at others bestowing on humankind the gift of fire, light, or food.

To this day Raven is a central figure in the richly imagined tribal arts of the region. He is depicted, along with other important animal spirits, in a highly stylized form on totem poles, carved boxes and utensils, jewelry, weavings, and baskets.

This tale is told with variations throughout all the native groups of the northwest coast. Within its dreamlike setting, Raven balances his heroism and trickery to bring a blessing to the people.

—G. M.

For Trevor, Erin, and Caitlin

aven came.

All the world was in darkness.
The sky above was in darkness.
The waters below were in darkness.
Men and women lived in the dark and cold.

Raven was sad for them.
He said, "I will search for light."

Raven flew across valleys and across mountains.
He flew along rivers and over lakes. There was
darkness all around.

Then he saw a bit of light far away.
He flew and flew and came closer to the light.
The light was at the edge of the water.

The light came from the house of the Sky Chief, and it was shining.
Raven perched high in a pine tree on the shore.
Raven watched.

He saw a beautiful young girl
emerge from the shining house
and go to the edge of the water.

She was the Sky Chief's daughter.
She knelt and drank some water from
a woven basket.

Raven changed himself into a pine needle.

He fell down from the tree
and floated on the water.

When the girl drank again, she swallowed the pine needle.

After a time, the girl gave birth to a child.
The child was small and dark with shiny
black hair and tiny black eyes.

Who do you think the child was?

It was Raven.
Raven had been reborn as a boy child.

The Sky Chief was delighted with his daughter's child. He called him grandchild. He played with the boy and carved toys for him. He invited the elders to come and see the curious, wonderful child.

The elders gathered in the shining house with the Sky Chief and his daughter. They watched Raven-child crawl around the floor of the lodge. He pretended to be playing. All the time, he was trying to find where the light was hidden.

He saw a box in the corner
of the lodge.

The box was large.
It was carved and painted
with many colors.
The box was bright. It glowed.
Raven-child said, "Ga! Ga!"

"What do you want?" asked his mother.
Raven-child said, "Ga! Ga!" He began to cry.
"What does the child want?" asked the elders.
Raven-child said, "Ga! Ga!" He cried and cried.
"My grandchild wants the box," said the Sky Chief.

The young woman placed the box in front of Raven-child, but he continued to cry.

She took the lid off the box.
Inside was a smaller box.

She took the lid off that box.
Inside was a smaller box.

His mother took the lid off that box, and light
poured out of it. Light flooded the room.
Inside the box was a shining ball, blazing with light.

What do you think the ball was?

It was the sun.

"Give him the ball," said Sky Chief.

His mother gave Raven-child the ball.
Raven-child stopped crying.
He began to play with it.
He rolled it around the floor of the lodge.
"Ga! Ga!"

Then he changed into a bird.
"Ha! Ha!"

He became Raven once again.
"Caw! Caw!"

Sky Chief, his daughter, and the elders looked on in amazement. Raven plucked up the ball of light in his beak, flew through the smoke hole of the lodge, and disappeared into the dark sky.

Raven flew over the valleys and the mountains.
He flew along the rivers and across the lakes.

Raven threw the sun high in the sky,
and it stayed there.
This is how Raven stole the sun
and gave it to all the people.

And why do the people always feed Raven?

To thank him for bringing them light.